THE ADDVENTURES OF PLUSMAN

WRITTEN
AND
ILLUSTRATED

BY MICHAEL CHERRY

This book is dedicated to the mathematicians, engineers,
architects, scientists, chemists, physicists, accountants,
artists, teachers, carpenters, construction workers, cashiers,
and all of the people who use math everyday.

Special thanks to Tracy, Cameron, and Ben
for their help with multiplying.

5:46 A.M. SPHERE RISE. THE GEOMETRY OF A NEW DAWN. THE SUN PEEKS OVER THE HORIZONTAL. ITS RAYS ILLUMINATE A NEW DAY IN PLANEVILLE.

5:47

RRiN!

AURGH, GOTTA GET UP. TIME TO RISE AND RUN. MORNING'S ALWAYS AN UPHILL BATTLE, BUT IT'S BEST TO MAINTAIN A POSITIVE SLOPE.

TIME

SPACE

I KNOW MY HEAD FIT THROUGH HERE LAST NIGHT. HMMM, SAME CIRCUMFERENCE, SAME VOLUME. COULD I JUST BE SPACIER?

NEED COFFEE NOW!!!

ENERGY

A CYLINDER OF JUICE.

JAVA

OVALS OVER EASY

THE NATURE OF MATH

MEET MILD MANNERED ADAM TEGETTER, UNASSUMING GRAPHIC DESIGNER, AND ALL 'ROUND NICE GUY.

GOTTA GET TO THE ADD AGENCY.

WITH BUSINESS MULTIPLYING AND ALL OF THE NEW PRODUCT CAMPAIGNS, THEY'LL BE COUNTING ON ME.

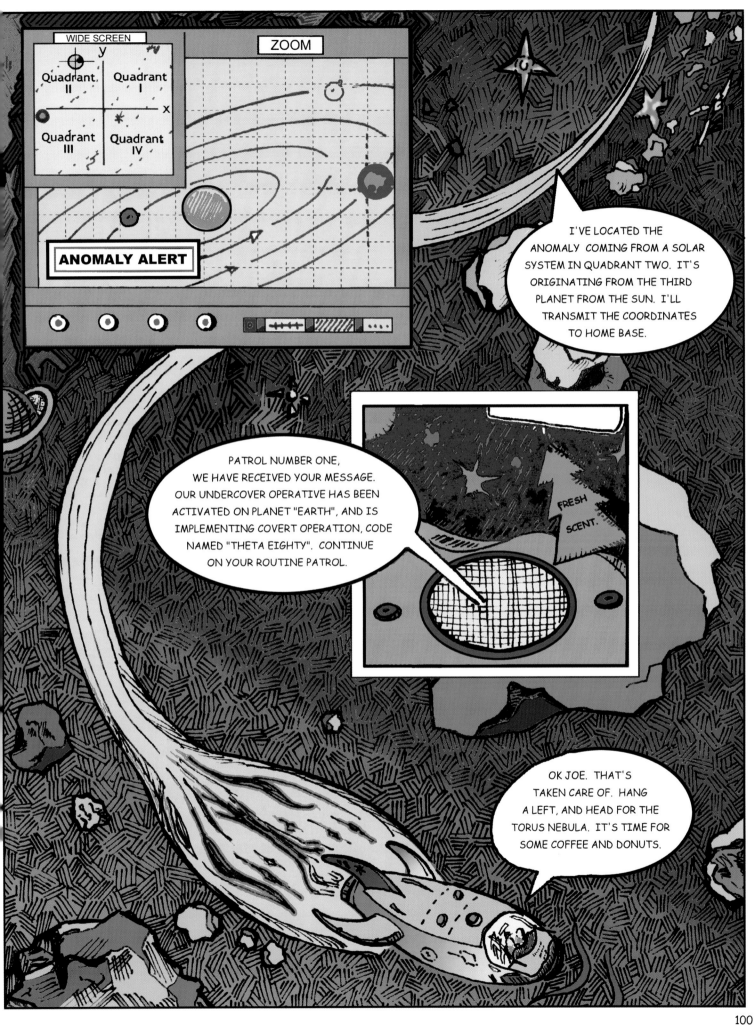

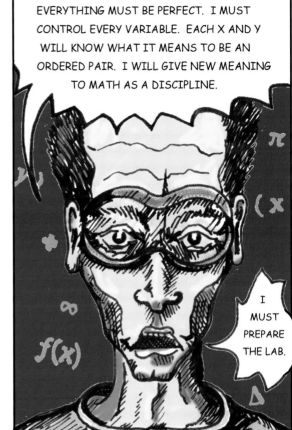

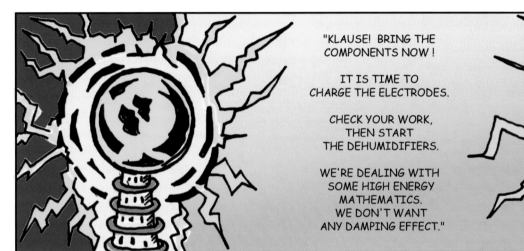

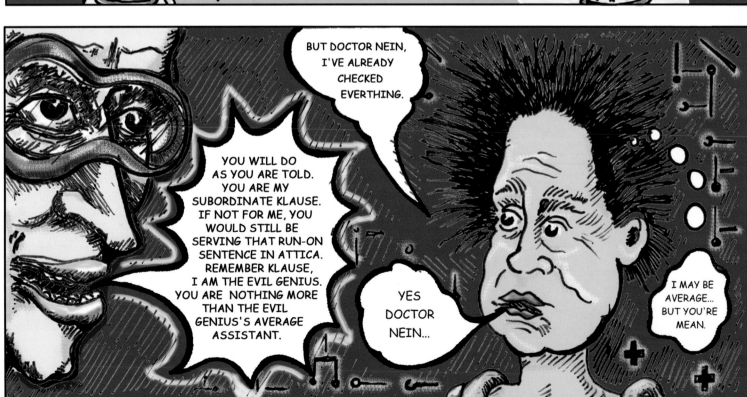

ADD WORLD, HERE I COME.

HEY, THAT'S AIDEE DEGRANGLE, THE NEW DESIGNER MR. HEDRON JUST HIRED. SHE MAY BE WORKING ON A NUMBER OF MY ACCOUNTS. SHE SURE IS A CUTE ANGLE.

I WONDER WHY SHE BRINGS HER DOG TO WORK. ODD, I DON'T RECOGNIZE THE BREED, AND IT ONLY HAS THREE LEGS.

OH NO! ANOTHER POWER OUTAGE, AND I'M STUCK IN AN ELEVATOR WITH AIDEE. GEEZ, I CAN'T SEE A THING, BUT I'VE GOT TO GET OUT OF HERE.

I KNOW TRIPOD. I HEAR WHAT YOU'RE SAYING.

WOOF! WOOF!

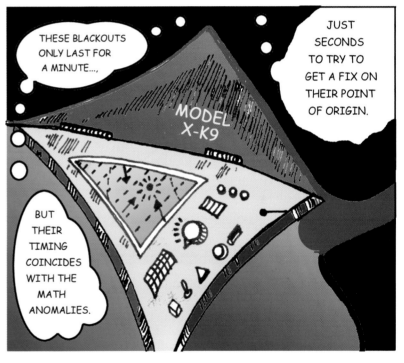

THESE BLACKOUTS ONLY LAST FOR A MINUTE...,

JUST SECONDS TO TRY TO GET A FIX ON THEIR POINT OF ORIGIN.

BUT THEIR TIMING COINCIDES WITH THE MATH ANOMALIES.

MODEL X-K9

ADAM! WHERE ARE YOU GOING? THIS ISN'T OUR FLOOR.

WOOF! WOOF

SHE'S GOING TO THINK I'M OBTUSE, BUT I CAN'T LET HER KNOW MY SECRET.

I KNOW, I'LL JUST TAKE THE STAIRS.

I GOT A VALUE FOR d BUT NOT ENOUGH TIME TO DETERMINE Θ WHAT SHOULD I DO NEXT? I LACK DIRECTION, AND I NEED TO COME UP WITH A NEW ANGLE IF I'M GOING TO BREAK THIS CASE.

I INTEND TO PURSUE OTHER INTERESTS AND TO EXPLORE TRANSCENDENTAL FUCTIONS. I HOPE TO FIND INNER PEACE OF MIND AND THE TRUE MEANING OF MATH.

YES TRIPOD, I TOO SENSE THAT THE MATH FORCE IS STRONG WITHIN HIM.

BOW WOW WOW !

HMMM... IF THERE'S A NEW (f) HEX THEN THAT OPENS UP A WHOLE NEW RANGE OF POSSIBILITIES FOR ME....

WITH MY DEPARTURE, THE ADD AGENCY WILL BE GETTING A NEW ART DIRECTOR, A PERSON TO TAKE THE AGENCY IN THE DIRECTION IT NEEDS TO GO. WITH THE CHANGES, YOU'LL BE GETTING MORE RESPONSIBILITIES. WE JUST GOT A BIG NEW ACCOUNT FROM A COMPANY CALLED LIVE X. YOU'LL BE MEETING WITH THE CEO OF THE COMPANY, A DOCTOR NEIN, TODAY AT NOON.

THIS IS THE FILE ADAM. GOOD LUCK...

...AND ADAM YOU'LL BE REPORTING TO AIDEE. SHE'S THE NEW ART DIRECTOR. SHE KNOWS DIRECTION AND RECOGNIZES THE MAGNITUDE OF THE JOB. GIVE HER ALL THE HELP YOU CAN.

TEN DEGREES AIDEE.

THANK YOU ADAM.

I SUPPOSE THAT A COMPLEMENT WAS IN ORDER.

HEX THOUGHT AIDEE EMBODIED DIRECTION AND MAGNITUDE BETTER THAN I DO. OH WELL. TO THE VECTOR GO THE SPOILS.

HEX A. HEDRON DIRECTOR

STILL, ON THE POSITIVE SIDE, THIS IS THE BIGGEST ACCOUNT I'VE EVER HAD!

LATER AT THE LIVE X CORPORATE H.Q.

THIS MUST BE THE SPOT.

MEANWHILE, INSIDE HIS LAB ON THE NINTH FLOOR OF THE LIVE X BUILDING DOCTOR NEIN CONTINUES WITH HIS CONQUEST OF MATHEMATICS.

SLOWLY WITHIN THE MATH PLASMA A SHAPE BEGINS TO COALESCE AND THEN A SOUND...

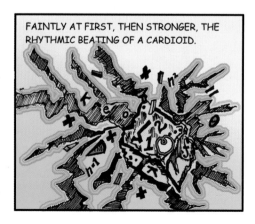

FAINTLY AT FIRST, THEN STRONGER, THE RHYTHMIC BEATING OF A CARDIOID.

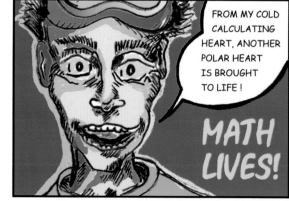

FROM MY COLD CALCULATING HEART, ANOTHER POLAR HEART IS BROUGHT TO LIFE!

MATH LIVES!

WHAT IS IT DOCTOR?

I HAVE TAKEN LIFELESS NUMBERS, SYMBOLS AND FORMULAS, UNITED THEM WITH LIMITLESS CREATIVITY, AND BOUNDLESS CURIOSITY. THE RESULTING MATH CUBE EMBODIES THE INFINITE POSSIBILITIES OF MATH. KNOWLEGDE IS NOT ENOUGH. POWER COMES WITH THE ABILITY TO UTILIZE AND MANIPULATE KNOWLEDGE.

DOCTOR... WHY IS THE CUBE GROWING SO QUICKLY?

THE COMPLEXITIES OF MATH THAT MAKE IT DIFFICULT, ALSO MAKE IT INTERESTING. GROWTH COMES WITH INTEREST, AND EVERYONE KNOWS THAT INTEREST COMPOUNDS EXPONENTIALLY. NOW QUICKLY TO THE 57 CHEVY!

I'LL DERIVE. YOU USE THE REAR DIFFERENTIAL TO REDUCE THE POWER OF THE CUBE. I WILL CONTROL IT!

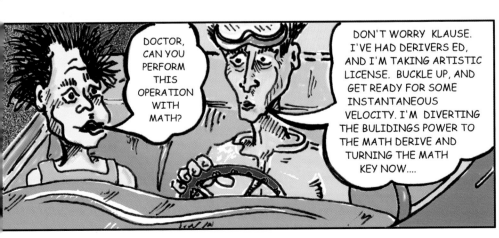

DOCTOR, CAN YOU PERFORM THIS OPERATION WITH MATH?

DON'T WORRY KLAUSE. I'VE HAD DERIVERS ED, AND I'M TAKING ARTISTIC LICENSE. BUCKLE UP, AND GET READY FOR SOME INSTANTANEOUS VELOCITY. I'M DIVERTING THE BULIDINGS POWER TO THE MATH DERIVE AND TURNING THE MATH KEY NOW....

HERE I GO. I'VE GOT TO MAKE A GOOD FIRST IMPRESSION.

I CERTAINLY HOPE THAT DOCTOR NEIN IS A NICE GUY.

I HATE SMALL PLACES. WHY DO THEY HAVE TO MAKE ELEVATORS SO CONFINING?

OH NO......
NOT AGAIN....

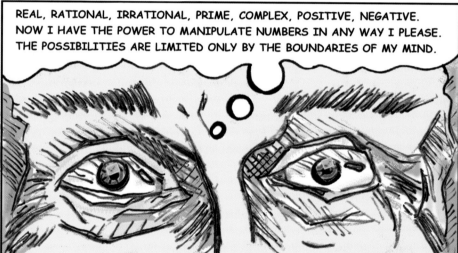

CONDUCTED BY THE MOISTURE IN THE AIR, FREED FROM THE CONFINES OF THE CUBE, WAVES OF MATH ENERGY SPILL INTO THE LAB. THEIR OCILLATIONS, THOUGH DAMPED, DRIVEN BYTHE LAB'S ELECTRODES, INCREASE IN AMPLITUDE UNTIL THEY REND THE VERY FABRIC OF THE MATH SPACE TIME CONTINUUM AND OPEN A RIFT BETWEEN OUR UNIVERSE AND ONE OF PURE MATH. THE LAB IS REFORMATTED, AS ARE THOSE INSIDE IT. THE RESULTS ARE SHOCKING.

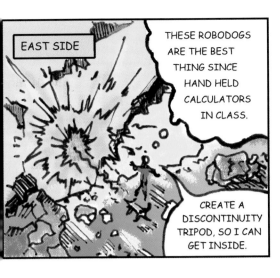

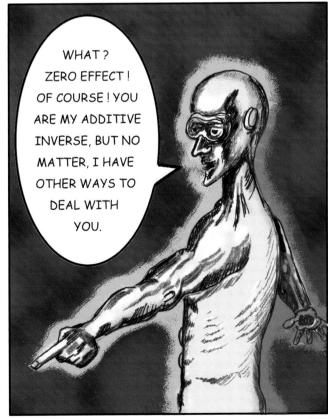

10010

UH-OH, THAT'S A LARGE NEGATIVE EXPONENT. IF HE HITS ME WITH THAT, I'LL BE A SMALL FRACTION OF THE MAN I WAS.

CAN'T LET MYSELF PANIC, CAN'T LET MATH ANXIETY GET THE BEST OF ME. THERE'S NOTHING TO FEAR BUT THE SPHERE ITSELF.

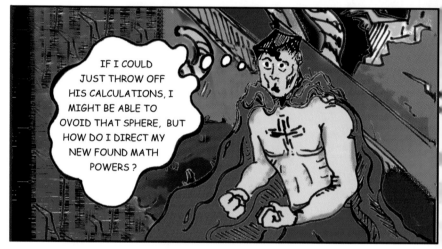

IF I COULD JUST THROW OFF HIS CALCULATIONS, I MIGHT BE ABLE TO OVOID THAT SPHERE, BUT HOW DO I DIRECT MY NEW FOUND MATH POWERS?

WHOOSH!

WHO HAS BROKEN THE BASE OF MY EXPONENT!

WHAT?

WHO DARES REDUCE THE POWER OF THE PERMUTAION?

I DO.

AND JUST WHO ARE YOU?

AGENT THETA EIGHTY.

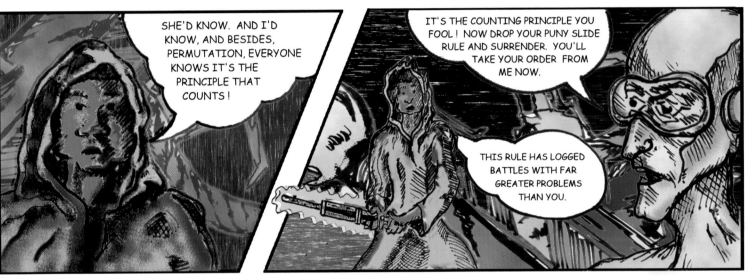

notes

Who knows what lurks in the hearts of true Muth enthusiasts!

MY FIRST
SKETCH OF
ADAM TEGETTER

sketches